PETER POWERS™

and the Sinister Snowman Showdown!

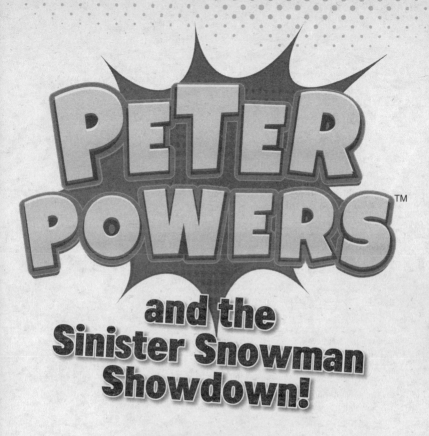

PETER POWERS™

and the Sinister Snowman Showdown!

By Kent Clark
& Brandon T. Snider
Art by Dave Bardin

SCHOLASTIC INC.

ISBN 978-1-338-26357-2

12 11 10 9 8 7 6 5   22 23

Printed in the U.S.A.   40

First Scholastic printing, November 2017

Cover and interior art by Dave Bardin
Cover design by Christina Quintero

Photos ©: cover burst: Studio_G/Shutterstock

Contents

CHAPTER ONE
Holiday Jinx

"Put your hands in the air and step away from the Christmas tree!" Mom ordered. My siblings and I scattered in all directions. We definitely didn't want to upset her. The fate of our presents was at stake!

After dinner, the air thickened with the sweet smell of fresh-baked cookies. Mom had just finished whipping up a batch, and they smelled *delicious*. The scent drove Dad wild. But other than the tree and the cookies, our family celebrated the holidays a little differently from other people: It was *Chrismukkah* in the Powers household.

Mom grew up celebrating Christmas. And Dad grew up celebrating Hanukkah. When they got married, they decided to smash both holidays together into one big festival of lights and presents as a way of honoring everyone's favorite traditions.

Oh, before I forget: My name is Peter. And did I mention that everyone in my family has superpowers?

"I thought you said these boxes were *heavy*," my little sister, Felicia, said. She carried a dozen giant boxes of decorations into the living room like it was nothing.

Felicia has super strength. She can bench-press a boat.

My older brother, Gavin, dove into the boxes like a maniac, pulling out clumps of tangled holiday lights. "This'll be *my* mission!" he said. He snapped his fingers twice, and each time a brand-new Gavin appeared out of nowhere. Gavin's power is making copies of himself. And all of them are as annoying as the original. The three Gavins untangled the lights.

In the corner, Dad lit the menorah candles with one fingertip. He has the power to make fire, so everyone calls him Fireman. Mom is called Flygirl (even though she isn't a girl anymore). Mom can soar through the sky like a fighter jet. Together, Mom and Dad are Boulder City's favorite superheroes.

"Candles all lit!" Dad said.

"Honey, aren't you supposed to light only one of the candles on the first day?" Mom reminded him.

"Ooooopsie! Good call, sweetheart,"
Dad said. He waved his hand across all
but one of the flickering menorah candles
and sucked each tiny flame back into his
palm.

"*Whoa!*" I said. "What did you just
do? I knew you could *make* fire, but I've

never seen you *take fire away*. How'd you do it?"

"I control fire. So if I concentrate hard enough, I can pull the heat back in," Dad said. "Cool, huh?"

"I wish *I* could do that," I said. Of everyone in my family, my superpowers are the lamest. I can create ice cubes. I freeze stuff too, on occasion. I've been trying to strengthen my powers. Some days it feels like I'll never become the superhero I dream of being. Mom says I'm her "little snowman," but I'm ready to be "the Winter Storm"! (Okay, so I haven't figured out my superhero code name, but I'm working on it....)

"The keys to growth are focus and

commitment. That's how you discover new abilities," Dad explained.

"Let me try," I said, making a small ice cube in my hand. Then I concentrated with everything I had—but I couldn't absorb the ice cube.

"Give it time, Peter," Dad said. "These things happen when you least expect them."

Mom brought a plate of fresh cookies into the living room. "They're still warm. Be careful," she said. "Where's Grandpa?"

"*GEEEEEEEEEEEEEEEEEEEEE!*" My brother Ben's joyful noise traveled down the hallway. He was riding on Grandpa's lap as they both zoomed around in Grandpa's wheelchair.

"I'm pooped!" Grandpa said, wheeling to a stop. He sniffed little Ben's rear end and scrunched his nose. "And from the smell of it, so are you!"

Ben can turn invisible—which makes babysitting a big pain. (How do you watch an invisible kid?) Grandpa is a retired superhero, but every time I see him, he's using a new power. He sprouts giant wings, possesses super eagle-eye vision, and even has a long tongue for eating bugs. (Gross!) I think he keeps his abilities a secret on purpose. I wonder what other things he can do.

"It's snowing!" I screamed, running to the window. My siblings and I were hoping for a snow day so we could get out of going to school the next day. (Sure, it was the last day of school before the holiday break, but a day off was a day off.) Now that small white flurries were gently falling, it looked like we might get our wish.

"*Nothing* is going to ruin this holiday," I said.

Gavin slapped me on the back of my head. "Way to *jinx* things, jerk!" he said. "Saying something like that just invites bad luck."

CHAPTER TWO
Snow Day!

"NOOOOOOOO SCHOOOOOOOOOL!"
Felicia howled.

The storm had turned into a full-on
blizzard overnight. The whole town
was covered in two feet of fluffy white
snow. Outside, a winter wonderland was
waiting to be explored. I got excited. Cold
weather was my thing, after all.

I sneaked into Gavin's room to deliver
the good news. He was still sleeping. I bent
over and yelled in his ear, "School's closed!"

Gavin threw a pillow at me and mumbled, "Then let me sleep, turd-burger."

"Jinx, schminx." I laughed to myself. I laced up my snow boots and bundled up tight. Technically, my ice powers made me immune to the cold, so I didn't need to wear a coat. But I still wore one to look stylish. That, and Mom said it helped to keep my secret identity secret.

At the park, folks from all over town were making snowmen, snow angels, and snow forts. I met up with my best friends, Chloe and Sandro.

"Look at all this beautiful powder!"

I exclaimed, scooping up some snow and tossing it into the air. "It's *perfect*."

"Don't eat the *yellow* snow!" Sandro warned. "It's *not* lemonade-flavored." He was the funny one in our trio, and his appetite was legendary.

"Sandro, everyone knows that," Chloe said, rolling her eyes and giggling. "But it's odd how this blizzard came out of nowhere. Not that I'm complaining. One extra day in our holiday break is awesome—still, it's worth noting." Chloe was a genius wherever she went.

"Who wants to build a snowman?" Sandro asked, diving into a pile of white fluff. We gathered up snow and crafted the coolest trio of snowmen. We used tree branches to make their arms, and rocks for their eyes. Chloe gave her snow*girl* a Mohawk, and I made mine into a lion with a mane of icicles.

"Look at them," I said, proud of our

work. "Someday I'll command an army of snowmen just like this, and together we'll save the universe!"

"Don't get ahead of yourself, Peter," Chloe said. "You've got a while before that happens."

Don't I know it, I thought.

"How should I decorate mine?" Sandro asked, pointing at his faceless snowman. "He looks sad. And kind of scary." Sandro grabbed a dirty old baseball cap from the park trash and put it on the snowman's head. "Nice, right?" he said. The hat was totally gross, but Sandro didn't care. I took my gloves off and put them on the end of his snowman's stick arms.

"He needs something else," Chloe said. "One more thing."

In my pocket, I felt something weird— a golf ball from putt-putt last winter. I'd totally forgotten where I put it. "Time for the finishing touch," I said, using the blue golf ball as the snowman's nose. "*Now* he's *perfect*."

"We should call him Blizzy Bliz! You know, after the blizzard," Sandro suggested. As we high-fived each other, a snowball smacked Sandro right in the face. We were under attack!

"You thinking what I'm thinking?" Sandro grinned.

"SNOWBALL FIGHT!" all three of us yelled. Chloe and I ducked down to start making snowballs. Sandro surveyed the park, watching the snowballs fly back and forth. "We have four different teams to take down," he said.

The excitement of the snowball fight and the chill in the air gave my powers an extra boost. I felt a jolt of frosty energy move through my body toward my hands. I focused my powers and...*plop! plop! plop!* Three soft, grapefruit-sized snow-balls formed in my hands.

"One for each of us!" I shouted. My friends and I took aim and threw, lobbing the snowballs at our enemies. The park was filled with laughing people having fun playing in the snow. It was amazing. Best. Snow Day. Ever.

CHAPTER THREE
Santa Claus & Krampus's Claws

Piles of wet clothes and boots were scattered next to the front door. It had been a very successful snow day. Now my brothers, sister, and I were relaxing with Mom in the living room, telling her all about the day's adventures. Dad was out doing the superhero thing. He was helping clear the roads of dangerous ice while we were inside drinking hot chocolate.

"You should have seen the park. Everyone built a snowman. It was like a whole army of snowpeople," I told Mom. "I even used my powers to make snowballs!"

"Be careful with your powers," Mom said, bouncing Ben on her knee. Then she added, "When I was little, I loved making snow angels."

"*Lame!*" Gavin laughed. "Angels are dumb. Snow *monsters* are better."

"Goes to show you've never met a snow monster before. You wouldn't stand a chance against *Krampus*," Grandpa said. "He'd eat you all for breakfast and burp each of you back up, one by one."

"Gross," said Felicia, scrunching her nose. "And what's a *Krampus*?"

"You don't know?" Grandpa's eyes

widened. "He's Santa's evil cousin. Claus rewards little girls and boys with presents for being good. But Krampus

punishes them with his terrible claws for being bad. Who do you think will visit *you* during Chrismukkah?"

"Krampuzz!" Ben giggled.

"Santa is just an old myth parents use to make kids behave," Gavin grumped. "Santa's not real."

Grandpa grabbed Gavin by the ear. "Santa is very real," he said. "He and I fought together back in World War II. He's a good soldier, with a huge appetite. And quite a cardplayer. Uh-oh, I think I owe him twenty bucks."

Mom kept checking her phone every few seconds. She looked almost nervous.

"Is everything okay, Mom?" I asked.

"Yeah, of course. It's just...Well, your father was supposed to be back hours ago," Mom said. "Using his flame power to melt the ice on the roads usually doesn't take this long. He should have at least checked in by now."

"Maybe he's helping *Santa* with our presents," Felicia said sarcastically.

"Or Krampus got him!" Gavin laughed.

Grandpa growled at them until they stopped.

"I'm sure everything's fine," Mom said.

But as the night went on, I began to worry too. The temperature was dropping fast. It was way too cold for Dad to be outside, even with his fire power to keep him warm. What if Gavin was right? What if I did jinx the holiday?

CHAPTER FOUR
The Search Begins

Felicia opened the front door and yelled, "DAAAAAAAAAAD! ARE YOU OUT THERE?!" Apparently, being super strong also meant being super loud. She was so loud that all the windows rattled.

"Felicia, stop yelling!" Mom said. "And close that door. You're letting in the cold!"

Grandpa swooped in to help. "You kids run upstairs and get into your jammies. Your mom can tuck you in while I take care of little Ben. Get moving, you filthy animals," Grandpa said, wheeling after Gavin and Felicia. They raced upstairs, tripping over each other as they went. Grandpa took Ben to his room for a diaper change. Mom and I were left alone. I needed to help her feel better.

"Dad probably lost his cell phone while saving the city. That kind of thing happens when you're a superhero, right?" I said. "Or his phone got eaten. I mean, I don't think *he* got eaten, or anything—"

Why did you say that? I thought. *Stop talking, you're not helping!*

Mom chuckled. "Heroes put their lives on the line all the time. You'd think I'd be used to this by now," she said. "Dad will be home in the morning, cooking some breakfast just like he always does. Don't worry, okay?"

"Okay," I said, before going up to bed. Mom told me not to worry, but I knew that's what she was going to do. After a lot of tossing and turning, I finally drifted off to sleep.

• • • • • • • • • •

The next morning, I woke up early. I lay in bed until I remembered Dad. Surely he was making breakfast downstairs. I ran down as fast as I could.

"Dad?!" I shouted. Instead, I found Mom asleep at the kitchen table. She must have been up all night waiting for Dad to get home. But he wasn't here.

"Peter, no shouting, please," Mom said, yawning.

"I'm sorry," I whispered. "No word from Dad?"

"No. I'm going to get dressed so I can look for him," she said, shuffling off to her bedroom in a daze.

Grandpa must have heard me shouting too, because he zoomed into the kitchen like a race car. "What happened? Is your dad back? What's going on?!?!" he asked. Gavin and Felicia arrived shortly after.

"WHA? WHERE? HUH?" babbled Gavin. He had some serious bedhead.

"Where's Dad?" Felicia asked.

"No one knows," I said. All of us sat quietly until Mom emerged in her superhero costume. It was on backward. I didn't have the heart to tell her. "I'm going to fly around the city, see if I can find your dad," she said.

"Can I brew you a fresh cup of coffee?"  I asked. "I also make a mean piece of toast. You should really eat something. Breakfast is the most important meal of the day. A very special mom once told me that." I forced a big smile.

"Why don't you just kiss her butt, Peter?" Gavin hissed at me.

"Shut your trap," I growled. "Can't you see she's worried?"

Mom gave herself a little slap on the cheek to wake up. "That's better," she said, shaking her head vigorously. "Thank you for the offer, Peter, but I'd rather you help Grandpa. Ben is still sleeping. Keep an eye on things while I'm out."

"No problem," I said.

Felicia and Gavin groaned. Mom kissed everyone on the cheek, then flew out the door. Gavin immediately snatched a box of cereal from the cabinet and poured it directly into his mouth.

"What's the big deal? Dad's fine," Gavin smacked, talking with his mouth full. "He's probably fighting shadow demons in Japan or something."

"Or saving a dragon princess in another dimension," Felicia said.

"Look, I know our parents always come home, but being a superhero is dangerous. Something bad could have happened. He may need our help. What do you say? The Powers Kids to the rescue?"

"No way," Felicia said. "Too cold outside."

"What she said," Gavin said.

I gazed out the window as a pep talk

began to form in my head. "Listen up!"
I said, turning around dramatically. But
Gavin and Felicia had left the room and
Grandpa was napping peacefully in
his wheelchair. I wasn't going to let any
of that stop me. It was time to call for
backup.

CHAPTER FIVE
The Snowman Question

Chloe, Sandro, and I spent all afternoon searching for Dad. (I'd asked my friends for help once my brother and sister proved useless.) We'd looked high and low but hadn't found a single clue. It was as if Dad had disappeared completely. I wasn't about to give up hope, though.

"Over here!" Sandro shouted. He'd found something in the snow. Chloe and I ran to check out his findings. "Oh, wait. Never mind," he said, shrugging his shoulders. "It's just a pile of trash cans. How did I think that was your dad?! I guess I need a sandwich."

"Gavin and Felicia should be here!" I said, stomping down the street in a huff. "He's *their* dad too. They act like it's no big deal that he's missing, but it's *really serious!*"

Chloe gave me one of her famous looks. It's the one that makes me realize I'm shouting when I should really be using my inside voice. "Your siblings are probably in denial. A missing dad is a lot for a person to take in. Ease up on them," she said. "Let's check out the park and look for clues."

GUUUUUUUUURRRRRRRRRGLE!

"We better hurry," Sandro said. "I can't control my stomach; it controls me."

We arrived at the park and found it eerily quiet. "Hey, is it just me, or is something missing here?" Sandro asked, scratching his head.

"ALL THE SNOWMEN ARE GONE!" I said.

"Why would someone steal snow-people?" Sandro asked. "They could just make their own."

"There are hundreds of footsteps in this park," Chloe said, bending down to inspect the frosty ground. "There's no way to figure out what happened."

"Does that mean Blizzy Bliz is dead?" sniffled Sandro. "I'm going to miss you, old friend. To some you were just snow, but to me, you were a hero. Speaking of *heroes*, do you guys like *sandwiches*? I do."

Chloe shushed Sandro. Now was not

the time to talk food. Dad was gone. All the snowmen were gone. Was there a connection between the two? Nothing made sense.

"Let's just go home," I said, defeated. Searching for a missing superhero dad was tougher than we imagined. It was time to call it a day. As we made our way through the neighborhood, I stared at my feet. What was I going to tell Mom? I thought I'd be coming home with good news.

Suddenly, Sandro said, "Blizzy Bliz! You're alive!" Sandro ran over to the snow-man and gave him a big hug. "You're not really *alive*, but you know what I mean."

When I looked up, I noticed something

very bizarre. The snowmen from the park had mysteriously reappeared! But now they were spread out among everyone's yards. It was as if someone had picked them up and moved them.

"I don't understand what's happening," I said. "The snowmen were in the park yesterday and now they're here. How did that happen? It's impossible!"

Then I spotted my brother through the living room window. He and one of his copies were playing video games. If Gavin made enough copies of himself, they could probably move all the snow-men on their own as a prank.

"*Not* funny," I murmured. While I was trying to find Dad, my brother was up to no good.

CHAPTER SIX
Family Matters

"I didn't do it!" Gavin snapped.

"Yeah, right," I said.

Dinner was tense. Mom was concerned about Dad. Felicia was secretly playing with her phone under the table. Ben refused to eat. And Gavin pretended like he didn't know how the snowmen got in everyone's front yards. I didn't believe him. The only person I wanted to talk to was Grandpa, but he was dozing off in his wheelchair.

After dinner, I made Mom a cup of hot chocolate.

"OUCH!" Mom said, fanning her mouth. "This is some *very* hot chocolate."

"Sorry about that," I said, holding out my palm. I created a tiny little ice cube and plunked it into Mom's drink. "That should cool it off."

Mom was impressed with how good I'd become at using my power. I was too. Soon her beverage was safe to drink. Crisis averted!

"You're becoming quite the expert at making ice these days." Mom smiled. "My little guy is growing up. One day you'll be a hero."

"I wish that day was today. Then I would have caught Gavin moving the snowmen. Gavin probably created a fleet of duplicates to do it. Maybe Felicia helped, using her super strength!"

"What if it wasn't your brother and sister?" Mom asked.

"It definitely was," I said. "Did you see the creepy snowman in our front yard? It looks like he's angry."

"You're the only snowman in my life," Mom said, rubbing my head. We heard a shuffling sound and turned to find that Grandpa had entered the kitchen. He was fully dressed to go outside. And he was standing!

"Dad! What are you doing out of your wheelchair?" Mom asked.

"The old knees are having a good day," Grandpa huffed. He zipped up his jacket and adjusted his hat. "Now I'm going out to look for that husband of yours, and I'm not coming back until I find him. Don't wait up!"

Mom wasn't having any of Grandpa's nonsense. "You're not going anywhere," Mom said. "It's freezing outside!"

"I may not be the man I used to be, but I'm still your *father*. You need a break. Let me take over the search for a bit. I can handle the cold. I'm a superhero too, you know!" Grandpa said. "If anyone can find that guy of yours, it's me. Remember, I've got the *nose of a dog*."

"Since when?" I asked.

Grandpa and Mom shared a sly smile. Then Grandpa kissed Mom on the cheek, tipped his hat in my direction, and opened his wings. Outside, he took off into the night sky.

"Does Grandpa really have a dog's sense of smell?" I asked.

"Your grandpa is full of surprises," Mom answered.

The dirty dinner dishes were piled up in the sink. I decided to wash them so Mom could go rest. I was scrubbing away when I looked out the kitchen window and saw a pair of evil eyes staring back at me.

"*AGHHH!*" I shouted. A dozen ice cubes popped out of my fingers.

When I looked again, I could see Sandro's favorite snowman staring at me through the glass. I knew exactly who was behind this trickery. I stormed up to Gavin's room. "Quit moving those snowmen to freak me out!"

"What are you talking about?" Gavin asked. Tears welled up in his eyes. I'd never seen him look so frightened. Chloe was right. I was so upset that I didn't think about how my siblings were dealing with Dad's disappearance. It was just as tough on *them* as it was on Mom and me. Our emotions were in a big, crazy jumble.

"Are you okay?" I asked.

"I didn't do *anything*, I swear," Gavin said. His lip quivered as a tear fell down his cheek. "I'm too worried about Dad to be pulling pranks."

I grabbed my brother and hugged him tightly. Sometimes we didn't get along, but I was always there for him no matter what.

"I mean, there's a stack of presents downstairs," Gavin said, "and normally, I'd be down there shaking every single one trying to figure out what's inside. But right now, I don't even care about presents! I just want Dad to come home."

Then he added, "I bet I get socks this

year. Ugh. I hate getting socks as a present. It's the worst!"

Some things never change, I thought.

"Don't worry. Everything is going to be okay," I assured my brother. I'd heard that line a million times before, but this time I didn't know if I believed it.

CHAPTER SEVEN
Midnight Robbery!

"NOOOOOOOOOOOOO!" Felicia screamed.

The next morning, my sister's shrieks filled the house. "Is everything okay!?" I shouted, running down the stairs. Mom flew down after me.

Gavin and Felicia stood there like sad little penguins. Gavin pointed to the corner of the room. It was empty. I finally saw what all the commotion was about.

"The tree, the decorations, and all the presents—they're gone!" Felicia shouted. "Where did they go? Does this mean we're bad kids?"

I wanted to say yes, but I kept my mouth shut. It wasn't the right time for *that* discussion.

"Who cares about presents?! WHERE'S DAD?!?" Gavin shouted.

We all went silent. No one knew what to say or do. Felicia sobbed quietly. Gavin gave her a big hug. I joined in. Mom wrapped her arms around all of us. It was a giant Powers family hug sandwich.

BUUUURRRRRRRPPPPPPPP! A stinky belch filled the air. We turned to see

Grandpa in the corner, patting little Ben on the back.

"Ben sure can burp, huh?" Grandpa said. "This one's a stinker too."

Felicia giggled. So did Gavin. Mom couldn't hold a straight face for long either. I tried to keep it together, but soon enough we were all cracking up. Grandpa kept burping Ben like he was a noisemaker. While we were all laughing, I noticed something—there was a teeny trail of water in the middle of the floor.

"Stop everything," I said, breaking up the party. "No one move!"

Everyone froze in place as I tiptoed around the living room, investigating the water. The streaks of moisture began by the fireplace—next to where our Chrismukkah tree had stood. "It looks as if someone dragged something wet through the living room…" I said. I followed the trail to the front door and noticed that it was cracked open.

"…then they escaped out the front door." I opened the door, hoping to catch someone in the act. Instead, I saw that the whole neighborhood was in total chaos!

Entire families stood in their front yards looking around. Some adults rushed from house to house in a panic. Others were on the phone with police. But in every yard, children wailed. What had happened?!

That's when I noticed—all the snowmen that had been here yesterday were gone. They had disappeared. I had no idea what was happening. I spotted Mr. Gortz, our neighbor, and waved him over.

"Mr. Gortz, what is going on?!" I asked.

"Everyone's been robbed, Peter," Mr. Gortz said. "All the holiday presents in town are gone! Looks like the holidays have been canceled!"

CHAPTER EIGHT
Snowmen Can't Jump

Everyone in Boulder City was freaking out. Who could rob every house in town on the same night? Who would do such a terrible thing?

Chloe and Sandro met me at the park to go over all the important clues. When we got there, we were surprised to see the snowmen. "They're back," Chloe said, shaking her head in disbelief. "But how?"

All the snowmen had returned to the park. They were standing in the exact

places they were in before. They all
looked the same, down to their perfect
smiles.

"There's Blizzy Bliz!" Sandro cheered.
"Hey, do you guys know where snowmen
put their money? In a *snowbank*! Man, I'm
funny!"

"Yeah, well, I'm *furious*!" I snapped.
"First the snowmen are *here*. Then the
snowmen are *in our yards*. Now they're
back *in the park again*!" I paced back
and forth. "Meanwhile, my dad is missing
and the whole town has been robbed. Are
these things connected?"

I was so worked up I thought I was
going to explode. I squeezed my fist as

tight as I could, and when I opened my palm, I'd created an ice cube. I was so angry I threw it at Sandro's favorite snowman, hitting it right in the face.

"Hey! Don't hurt Blizzy Bliz!" said Sandro. "He didn't do anything to you. With everything gone, he's all that's left of the holidays."

"Stop being so nice to him. He's just a stupid snowman!" I shouted. People in the park stared at me. I quietly sat down on the ground to collect my thoughts.

Chloe patted me on the back. "We're going to find your dad *and* solve this mystery. But right now isn't a good time to lose your cool."

She's right, I thought. *My cool is everything to me.*

"Very funny, Sandro," I said, looking up. "Way to change Blizzy's smile into a scowl."

"Huh?" Sandro said. "I didn't."

All three of us looked at his snowman. It had sticks for eyebrows, which pointed down and toward the center, making the snowman look angry.

"Don't joke around, Sandro," Chloe said.

"I'm not," Sandro said. "I swear, I didn't touch him."

"Do you think it's possible…" I started, "…that the snowman is ALIVE?!"

The idea scared the bejeepers out of me.

"No way. You're seeing things, dude," said Sandro. "One time, after I got a tooth pulled at the dentist's office, I thought I saw a dragon with fire breath. It was really just a lady with a lot of red hair. Relax, bud."

"It did it again!" I shouted, pointing at it. "Its arms were down, and now they're up. I swear! This snowman is moving every time we turn our backs."

"Snowmen can't move, though!" Sandro said. "They can't walk, they can't jump, and they certainly can't get mad....Can they?"

"I think Peter's right," Chloe said. "This is freaking me out. We should get out of here...."

"Agreed," I said. As the three of us left, I looked back. I couldn't be sure, but it seemed like all the snowmen had moved toward us.

CHAPTER NINE
Peter Gets Mad

At dinner, I wasn't hungry. I made little piles of peas and carrots but didn't actually eat them. Usually Mom would insist I eat my veggies, but tonight she let it slide. Felicia broke the silence, asking, "Is Dad going to be home soon?"

"I hope so." Mom smiled weakly. "We can't give up hope."

"We *won't* give up hope," Grandpa added. "Right now we need to stay strong.

And the Powers family is stronger than most. Am I right?"

Everyone nodded. I hoped Grandpa was right.

After we cleared the table, Gavin and Felicia came into the living room to watch *Glorf the Vampire Troll from Underspace*. I went to my room instead. I felt like I was onto something, but I couldn't quite put my finger on it. As I lay on my bed, thinking about where Dad might be, I heard a rustling sound outside.

I rushed to the window. The snowmen had returned! They were back in everyone's yards as if they'd never left. I rushed out of my room and down the stairs and snuck out the front door. The front porch light was bright, but a snowman stood at the edge of the shadows.

As I got closer, I realized it was Sandro's snowman, Blizzy Bliz. He stared at me with an angry look on his face.

"Well, well, well. Look who it is," I said, slowly circling the snowman. "You and your buddies think you're so smart, don't you? But I'm onto your tricks. You can't fool me." I glanced up and down the block. The snowmen stayed where they were, but they all seemed to be watching me and Blizzy. I leaned in close.

"Who sent you?" I whispered. He didn't respond. I raised my voice so he knew I meant business. "What do you want, punk?!" He didn't budge. It was time to get super serious. I looked the snowman square in the eye and asked, "Where are the presents and where's my dad, you big chunk of dirty snow?!"

He didn't answer. He didn't move. I looked around the neighborhood. None of the other snowmen had moved either. But when I looked back at Blizzy Bliz, he wore a mean smile instead of the angry look he'd had before.

I was both scared and annoyed. But I couldn't let fear stop me. I ran at the snow-man and pushed. He was made of three round balls of snow, each one smaller than the one under it. I pushed the top two off.

Now Blizzy Bliz lay in three crushed balls on my front lawn. I hovered over the defeated snowman. He looked so sad and broken, I almost felt bad about it.

"Well, that's what you get for ruining my holidays," I said.

I turned to go back into the house. I was almost to the door when—*THWACK!*—something cold hit the side of my head.

The snowball had come out of

nowhere. *This must be the work of some pesky hoodlums*, I thought to myself. *Wait until I give them a piece of my mind.* I turned around, expecting to see some classmates trying to be funny. Instead...

I screeched, "WHAT THE?!"

My made-of-snow enemy, Blizzy Bliz, had re-formed. He was standing upright, all three balls back in place, as if I had never pushed him down. He glared at me, his face forming a terrible scowl. Blizzy Bliz looked evil.

"GRRRRRRRRRRR!"

The snowman growled like a dog. I ran back inside and slammed the door and locked it.

CHAPTER TEN
The Boy Who Cried Snowman!

"The snowmen are coming!" I shouted as I ran into the living room. I stood in front of the TV to make sure I had everyone's full attention. "Everyone up, we have to bar the doors and windows!"

"Cut it out, Peter," Felicia whined. "I'm trying to watch TV."

"Yeah, pulling pranks right now is *not* cool," Gavin moaned.

"I'm calling a Powers family meeting. We need to talk about something that's happening outside. Something BIG. We could be in terrible danger," I warned them.

Mom overheard me talking to my siblings and popped her head out of the kitchen. She'd just finished baking a new batch of cookies and was bouncing little Ben in her arms. She said, "Let your brother and sister watch their show in peace, Peter. Come have a cookie with me."

Normally, "have a cookie with me" was music to my ears—but not on this day. There wasn't time for cookies. A great danger was just outside.

"Mom, I think the snowmen might

be alive, *and* I think they may have kidnapped Dad," I said. "They're also the ones who took all the presents and holiday stuff from everyone. And now they're back. *We* could be next."

My tone must have scared Ben, because he started crying. "Dah-dah?!" he wailed, squirming out of Mom's tight grasp. *"WAAAHHHH!"*

Mom wasn't pleased. "Peter, this isn't the time for one of your theories," she said, trying to comfort Ben as best she could.

"It's *not* a theory. The snowmen were in the park, then they were in our yards, then they were in the park again, now they're in our yards again," I rambled, "and one just hit me with a snowball!"

"*Enough!*" Mom said sternly. "I love you, Peter. I know you're worried. But jumping to wild conclusions is the wrong thing to do. Go to your room."

"But, but, but…" I stammered. "The snowman army is real!"

Ben's cries grew louder. "Peter, upstairs! Now!" Mom said.

I marched up to my room. As I changed into my pajamas, I decided to stay vigilant. If I had to, I would watch them from my window. From here, I could see everything happening in the neighborhood. The snowmen were staying put for the time being, but I didn't know how long that would last.

KNOCK-KNOCK-knock-KNOCK-knock-KNOCK! KNOCK KNOCK!

There was only one person who knocked on my door like that—Grandpa. He opened the door slowly, peeking in to see if I was asleep. "How you doing, Peter?" he asked. "I wanted to have a good old-fashioned chat with my favorite grandchild."

"You say that to all your grandkids," I reminded him.

"Yeah, but with *you*, I actually mean it." He laughed, taking a seat at the end of my bed. He pulled a napkin from his pocket.

Inside it were two fresh, hot cookies. He took one and offered me the other.

"Hey! How did you get up the stairs?" I asked. "I thought your knees started acting up again after you went out looking for Dad."

"I've got all kinds of tricks you haven't seen. Let's just say I *wormed* my way up." He laughed again. Sometimes I didn't get old people's jokes.

Then he turned serious. "Now, Peter, I've been around a long time. I've lived through a lot of nutty junk. I've seen robot squirrels, brain-eating aliens, power-stealing pirates, a blob of goo that can become anything imaginable—"

"That *is* a lot of weird stuff," I said.

"You said it!" Grandpa shook his head in disbelief. "My point is, *living* snowmen don't seem so crazy to me."

"Tell that to Mom," I said.

Grandpa chose his words carefully. "Your mom has a lot on her mind. There's no need to worry her more than necessary. How's this: Why don't we both keep our eyes peeled for trouble? If you see something out of the

ordinary, give a holler. And if I see something out of the ordinary, I'll give a holler."

It sounded like a simple plan to me.
"Okay, Grandpa," I told him. "I'm in."

Grandpa smiled. "This whole mess'll
get figured out soon enough, and your
dad will be home before you know it. Now,
keep those eyes open."

He patted me on the head and left. I
perched myself at my windowsill so I could
watch the snowmen. I was going to stay
up all night long if I had to. That's what
Dad would do in order to solve a mystery.

But as the night got later, my eyelids
grew heavier. Before I knew it, I had fallen
fast asleep.

CHAPTER ELEVEN
Frosty Frauds

"NO NO NO NO NO NO NO NO NO NO NO NO!" Felicia's shrieking from downstairs woke me up. Again.

But as I ran into the hallway, I collided with Felicia. "If it's not you screaming, then who is it?"

We ran downstairs to find Gavin in total shock. Mom flew downstairs, with Grandpa behind her, using his giant wings, and Ben in his arms. "*What is it?!*" they both shouted.

"We've been robbed—again! And this time, they took everything that is good in this world: cell phones, tablets, laptops, and even"—Gavin was about to cry—"our TV!!"

"How will I watch episodes of *Dr. Seymour Whiskerkins, MD*?" Felicia asked, collapsing onto the couch. "He's a kitty that's a doctor to other kitties. It's the cutest thing ever....*When did my life become a nightmare?*"

Once again, there were tracks of water all over the floor. "The snowmen did it," I said.

"Enough of that nonsense, Peter," Mom scolded. "I mean it. I don't want to hear any more of your crazy ideas. *Snowmen are not alive.*"

I couldn't understand why no one believed me. I was so frustrated...then suddenly I was shouting: "We live in a world with tornado captains, robot armies, spider ladies, and lizard people from the center of the Earth—how is it that the idea of *living snowmen* is too crazy for you?!"

Everyone just stared at me like *I* was the weirdo. "Fine, if you don't believe me, I'll go find proof!"

Once I solved the biggest mystery in Boulder City, they'd understand. I had to put my super sleuthing abilities to good use. I grabbed my coat and went to Chloe's and Sandro's houses. They'd been robbed too.

"Let's head to the park," I said. "If the snowmen are the thieves, everything they've stolen can't be far off, right?"

"They took every gaming console in my house," Sandro said sadly. "All eight of them." I forgot Sandro's family has tons of money.

"You'll get a new one, Sandro," Chloe said. "They took *my* game console, and I only had the one that I built from spare parts. It'll take me forever to build a new one."

We arrived at the park to see all the

snowmen back in their original locations. Not only that, they were wearing the evilest grins you could imagine. "Hey! That's my scarf!" Chloe yelled. She ran over to one of the snowwomen and yanked. The snowwoman's head fell off.

"That's right!" I said. "These nasty snowmen don't know they're about to experience the full PETER POWERS AND FRIENDS SMACKDOWN!"

"There's Blizzy Bliz!" Sandro said. "Get him!"

The three of us attacked. We ran up to our frosty enemy and looked him square in the eye. Then we tore him apart. "We're onto your tricks, you...slushy meanie!" I shouted. (Being a witty super-hero is harder than it looks.)

"EEEEEEEEEK!" Sandro shrieked, pointing to a different snowman. "*That* one just winked at me! It was a very evil wink."

"Let's get him!" Chloe yelled. She knocked him over.

"We'll stop if you tell us where my dad is!" I shouted.

"And all the town's stuff!" Sandro added.

"Silence, huh? Fine! That's it!" The three of us went around and knocked over all the snowmen.

"Oh no!" Chloe blurted, stumbling away from a threatening snowman. "Look!"

Suddenly we were surrounded by the snowmen. The second we turned our backs, they had rebuilt themselves. But how? Then we could hear the army of snowmen *whispering*. One of them even laughed! Another snorted.

"Man, I wish I had fire powers instead of cold powers," I said. "I'd melt these snowmen down into puddles. Then I'd stomp in those puddles just to show them who's in charge."

"Peter! That's it! That's the reason they took your dad," Chloe said. "Mr. Powers can control fire. He's a snowman's worst nightmare. Think about it."

"Chloe is right! Your dad could mop the

floor with these dudes. For REAL," Sandro said. "It's a shame he's the *only* person who can stop them."

"Maybe not," I said in my toughest-sounding voice. I was ready to confront the enemy once and for all. As I turned around to give those snowmen a piece of my mind, I tripped over my untied

shoelaces and fell into a pile of very yellow snow. The snowmen roared with laughter.

"You're all going to regret laughing at PETER POWERS!" I shouted, grabbing Chloe and Sandro and marching out of the park. I had a brand-new plan.

CHAPTER TWELVE
Stakeout!

Chloe, Sandro, and I had been watching the snowmen for hours. We'd pretended to leave the park so they'd *think* we'd gone. But we ended up hiding behind some thick bushes, out of sight. That way we could monitor the snowmen for suspicious activity and catch them in the act. Dad once told me that what we were doing was called a "stakeout."

But the snowman army just stood there in front of the woods behind the park. We could hear them whispering, but we never saw them move.

"I've got to pee," said Sandro. He did a little pee-pee dance to show us how bad he had to go. "And I'm bored and cold.... Can we go now?"

"Not yet," I said, peeking through the bushes. "Keep watching for trouble."

If we were going to take back Boulder City's holidays from a group of naughty snowmen, I needed to inspire my friends. I had to show them that I knew what I was doing. I had to be the leader I always dreamed of being. They needed to hear an inspirational speech!

FLUUUURRRRRRRRRPT!

Before I could speak, Sandro's stomach made a noise none of us had ever heard before. We couldn't tell if he was hungry or something worse.

"What was *that*?" Chloe asked.

Sandro was a little embarrassed. "It's dinnertime, you guys. I've got to get home," he confessed. "My stomach is *hangry*. It's about to eat itself."

"Peter, I don't want to bail, but I think I should go home too," Chloe said. "It's getting late, and the snowmen aren't moving."

"Don't go! We're on the verge of a breakthrough!" I pleaded.

"YOU GUYS!!!" Sandro hissed, motioning toward the snowmen. "THEY'RE GONE!"

"Darn it! We were only distracted for a minute. They couldn't have gone far," I said.

"There's some!" Chloe said, spotting the last few disappearing into the woods behind the park.

"I'm going after them!" I said.

"That's a terrible idea!" Chloe said.

"It's the only idea I've got," I said before getting up and following the snowmen.

As I approached the woods, I realized the sun was going down and it was getting dark. "I should have brought a flashlight," I said aloud.

"Good thing I did," Chloe said.

"What are you doing here?" I asked as my friends followed me into the woods.

"We're not going to let our best friend save the day without our help," Sandro said. "But you owe me dinner after this."

We walked deeper and deeper into the woods. Finally, we entered a clearing. It was stacked with TVs, stereos, computers, gaming consoles, and hundreds and hundreds of presents wrapped in holiday paper.

"I was right! The snowmen *are* the ones who stole all our stuff!" I yelled. I couldn't wait to rub it in my family's faces.

Chloe and Sandro screamed. I turned around to find my friends held prisoner by the sinister-looking snowmen.

"Drop my friends!" I yelled. "Or else!"

It was the perfect moment for me, Peter Powers, Ice King, to do his thing! (Okay, maybe not Ice King. I'm still experimenting with superhero names.) I stuck my hands out and began thinking chilly thoughts. My power ran through my body and showered the snow villains with ice cubes. I'd never made so many ice cubes in my entire life.

"OW! Knock it off, Peter!" Chloe said.

"Yeah, being pelted with ice doesn't hurt cold creatures, but it sure hurts us warm-blooded folks!" Sandro added.

The snowman army just laughed.

"Enough laughter!!" a deep, creepy

voice called out from the shadows. A hairy monster with two giant horns and a long red tongue stepped out into the clearing. He was the scariest thing I'd ever seen. (I may have even wet my pants a little. What? It happens!)

"Look what we have here," the creature said, licking his lips. "What *tasty little morsels* have been brought to *Krampus* this evening?"

Krampus, as in Santa's evil cousin? I thought. *We're all in trouble now.*

CHAPTER THIRTEEN
The Opposite of Santa

Krampus stood before me. He was covered in patches of matted hair, like he hadn't taken a bath in years. His hot, stinky breath lingered in the air.

Krampus was *real*. I couldn't believe my eyes. I thought he was just Grandpa's made-up story.

"I'm not a tasty little morsel!" I shouted at Krampus. "I'm Peter Powers, *Master* of *Ice*!" I hoped I sounded more confident than I felt.

SCHWACK!

A snowball hit my head. Ugh! Those snowmen loved to throw snowballs when your back was turned. The snowman army laughed at me. Krampus stalked toward me. He stank like the inside of a trash can. Yuck.

"I take it you're the big bad guy behind all this," I said. I'd watched enough superhero movies to know you should always get the villain to confess to his crimes before the big showdown.

"I am," Krampus said. His smile was all jagged, broken yellow fangs. Someone needed to brush more often.

"Why did you try to ruin the holidays?" I asked.

"Because I'm Santa's *evil* cousin," Krampus answered. "I'm evil!"

"You're also gross," I snarled.

Krampus giggled. "Perhaps, but thanks to my snowman army, I've got all the best stuff in town. Computers, TVs, toys, you name it. One house even had eight gaming systems. I took them all!"

"Hey! Those are mine," Sandro whispered behind me.

"So you turned those snowmen evil?" I asked Krampus.

"Nope." Krampus snickered. "*I* didn't turn those snowmen evil. They turned evil on their own. They were sick and tired of humans forgetting about them the minute the weather gets warmer. The sun comes out, they melt away, and *then* what? They wanted revenge. I simply gave them a purpose. To serve *me*."

"Why are you doing this?" I asked.

"WHY NOT?!" Krampus shouted. "My cousin may like to *give* presents, but I like to *take* presents!"

"And what about my dad? Did you take him too?" I asked.

"Your father? Oh, you mean my frozen-fire tree?!" Krampus pointed to the middle of the clearing. Two angry snowmen presented a big block of ice shaped like a Christmas tree. Dad was frozen inside it. Krampus laughed. "You want to help decorate him?"

Dad's body glowed. His fire power was the only thing keeping him alive inside the ice. But I didn't know how long that would last. I had to get him out of there quickly, but I didn't know how. My fingers were

tingling again. My power was growing stronger. But would my cold powers be any use against a winter monster? I guessed I'd have to find out.

"Let my dad go!" I yelled.

Then I opened my palms, pointed them at Krampus, and unleashed a fury of ice and snow like never before. Okay, maybe it wasn't *that* exciting, but there were definitely some flurries.

Krampus laughed. "You're not the only one with cold powers, kid." He opened his own hands, and huge gales of snow and icy wind pummeled me. Good thing I was immune to cold, or it would have frozen me solid.

"You've got some fight in you, kid. I like that. What if I told you there's a job for you in my new kingdom?" Krampus asked.

"What new kingdom?"

"I'm going to take over Boulder City

and turn it into a winter wonderland all
year round. I'm turning this place into an
EVIL SOUTH POLE."

"Boulder City isn't even in the Southern
Hemisphere," I said.

"I KNOW THAT!" Krampus screamed.
"But it's conveniently located near a
beach. Sometimes a snow monster just
wants to get away, you know?"

"No, I don't know," I said. "I'm not evil.
And I never will be."

Krampus glared at me. "Then you—like
the rest of your town—are *doomed*...."

CHAPTER FOURTEEN
Snowy Showdown

Krampus stomped toward me and grabbed me in his giant hands. "I can see your mind working, Peter. You've got to stop stressing out. You'll never beat me—so *join* me," Krampus said with a grin. "We can use our cold powers to rule this city. I'll help you develop them. We'll try all kinds of new things. Won't that be fun? Join me on a throne of ICE!"

"Never!" I shouted. I held up my hands

and pushed my powers as hard as I could. Dozens of ice cubes plunked out.

Krampus laughed. "You can't beat me, boy. You can't fight ice with ice. You need fire. And you've got none."

I looked at my dad, trapped inside the tree of ice. His powers of flame looked so dim now, like a candle about to go out....

THAT'S IT! I thought. Krampus had given me the idea of a lifetime. He didn't mean to, of course. Some villains can't help but talk so much that they give away the key to defeating them.

I pointed my hands at the big block of Christmas tree–shaped ice that imprisoned Dad. Then I thought of Dad and the menorah candles, and how he had said, "I control fire. So if I concentrate hard enough, I can pull the heat back in."

I took a deep breath and focused. I thought, *I control ice, so if I concentrate hard enough, I can pull the cold back in.*

"What are you doing, you little pip-squeak?" asked Krampus.

I was pulling all the cold into my body. The tree of ice began to chip and melt away. Dad's flame grew brighter as I grew colder.

"Stop! What are you doing?" Krampus cried.

"Learning a new trick," I said. "And once my dad is free, you're in for a big surprise!"

I finished absorbing the ice tree into my body, and Dad was finally free. He took one look around and shook his head.

"What is going on, Peter?" Dad asked. "Where am I?"

"I'll tell you the whole story over some of Mom's cookies," I said. "Right now, I need you to light up, burn bright, and melt everything in sight!"

Dad was dazed and confused but he trusted me. His eyes became a fiery red. His hands began to glow like little baby suns. The angry snowmen were about to attack. But Dad blasted them. Chloe and Sandro quickly jumped out of the way as Dad melted the snowmen into puddles. He took down the entire army in no time.

Krampus dropped me and began to run. Dad made a huge ring of fire surround the clearing so the monster couldn't escape.

"NO! NO! NO!" Krampus whined, falling to his knees in tears.

"I think you mean *HO! HO! HO!*" a cheerful voice called out from above. Jingle bells filled the air as a sleigh pulled by reindeer flew down from the sky. The jolly man commanding his sleigh wore red and had a big white beard. He was like a gleaming beacon of hope. He needed no introduction. It was SANTA CLAUS. He was REAL. Even *I* got chills.

Santa took one look at Krampus, shook his head in disappointment, and tossed a magic Christmas sack over him. "My magic sack should hold him." Santa laughed.

"You're *real*," I told Santa.

"Of course I'm real! I'm a superhero, just like your folks," Santa said. "Sure, I give out presents during the winter, but the rest of the year I stay trim by fighting crime. Please excuse my cousin. He's a

feisty fella! But you know how family is, am I right?"

Tell me about it, I thought.

"Thanks for saving the day, Peter," Santa said and smiled.

"MUMBLE-MUMBLE-MUMBLE-MUMBLE."

Krampus rolled around angrily inside Santa's magic sack. None of us could make out what he was saying, but it sure sounded mean. Santa tossed him into the back of his sleigh.

"I've got to get going, but thanks again for the assist. Sorry about all the trouble. Oh, and tell your grandpa Dale he owes me twenty bucks! And tell him not to be such a sore loser at our next game night," Santa said. Then he cracked the reins and took off into the sky. He shouted, "HAPPY CHRISMUKKAH TO ALL!"

Sandro and Chloe stood there with their mouths wide open. They couldn't believe what they'd just seen. I'll admit, I couldn't either.

"Was that who I think it was?" asked Sandro.

"Yep," I answered.

"Wow," Chloe said.

"I know that was Santa Claus and everything, but can you lend me a hand?" Dad asked. He was barely able to stand.

"Careful, Dad. You've been frozen for days. Let's get you home."

RUUUMMMBBBBLLLLEEE!

"What was that?" asked Dad. "I don't think I can handle any more evil snowmen."

"Just my stomach, Mr. Powers," Sandro said. "It needs food."

"Let's go home and eat cookies," Dad said. "I think we've all earned them."

CHAPTER FIFTEEN
Holiday Heat Wave

"Can we go swimming? PLEASE! It's Christmas Day!!!" Felicia begged. After Krampus and his evil snowman army left, the temperature in Boulder City went from winter to summer. We didn't know how long it was going to last, so we took advantage of it while we had the chance. Despite my love of ice, I was glad the snow had disappeared. It had become way more trouble than it was worth.

"The pools are closed," Mom reminded

my sister. "Everything was *frozen* a day ago! *Let it go*, Felicia."

Since it was so warm out, our family decided it would be way more fun to open presents in the backyard. We dragged them all outside for a little fun in the sun. We tore through the wrapping paper like animals.

"We still have one thing left to do," Mom said.

"More presents," Gavin and Felicia said at the same time.

"No," Mom said. "I know you kids think it's corny, but it's the most important part of the holiday and my favorite Chrismukkah tradition...."

"It's time to talk about what we're *grateful* for," said Dad. Gavin and Felicia moaned. "Okay, enough of that. Sharing what we're grateful for is important. Despite our differences, we should always remember how fortunate we are to have each other."

"What are you thankful for, Ben?" Grandpa asked.

"Trux!" Ben said, holding up his new toy.

"My turn!" Gavin said.

"After me," Felicia said, wrestling Gavin to the ground with one hand. "I'm grateful to have a good mom, a nice dad, two older brothers, one little brother, a funny grandpa, and a house to live in," said Felicia. "But I still wish we could go swimming."

"Now my turn!" Gavin said. "I'm grateful for all my new video games. Which, uh, I guess wouldn't be here if Peter hadn't used his lame powers to stop Krampus and save Dad. Or whatever."

"How about you, Peter?" Mom asked.

I could see Gavin and Felicia getting antsy. They thought I talked too much. I suppose they were right, but this time around I kept it short and sweet. "I'm grateful for the love and support of my family. I appreciate each and every one of you."

"UGH," Gavin moaned. "Peter's already trying to get on Santa's nice list for next year."

"*You* said you didn't believe in Santa," I said.

"Well, uh, um, I *didn't* think he was real," he mumbled. "But, you know, you and Grandpa and Dad have met him. So, I guess, you know, I believe now. You're still a kiss-up."

"Speaking of—Grandpa? Santa wants his twenty bucks," I said. "And he said not to be such a sore loser next time."

"Yeah, yeah, yeah. You think *I'm* a sore loser? Santa flips a table if he loses." Grandpa chuckled.

"I wish it was still snowing," Mom said. "It just doesn't feel like the holidays without it."

When I absorbed all the cold energy from the ice tree, I hung on to it. I still felt the frosty power inside me. I didn't know what to do about it. It was kind of like when you drink a fizzy soda. You've got all

the fizz inside you, making you want
to burp. So, I thought, why don't I let it
go and burp—or make it cold—like a
champion!

I grabbed the backyard water hose and
turned on the faucet. I shot the spray into
the air.

"Peter, are you crazy?!" Gavin said.

"Wait for it," Dad said, giving me a
wink. He knew what I was doing.

I let loose a super chilled blast of cold
energy and stuck out my tongue. A tiny
snowflake landed on the tip. Then another.
And another. Soon it was snowing in our
backyard like the most perfect holiday
ever—and it was all because of me. I'd

learned how to absorb *and* release cold power. It was so cool. Mom and Dad held hands and stared at each other with hearts in their eyes.

"Mom, Dad, Grandpa, you three need to say what you're thankful for," I noted.

"All of you," Mom said. She gave me a kiss on the cheek, then hugged us kids tight. Dad joined in, grabbing Grandpa and pulling him close. It was one big Powers family holiday hug sandwich.

"FAMIWEEEEEEEEE!" cooed Ben.

"That's right, kid," I said. *Family.*

KENT CLARK is a superhero by day and a writer by night. When he's not getting cats out of trees or saving the world from monstrous alien supervillains, he's reading a book. He also has a terrible weakness during the holidays—eggnog.

BRANDON T. SNIDER writes books about Transformers, Minions, and even Batman! When he's not writing superhero stories, he's either acting on TV or eating as much cheese as possible in order to unlock cheese-related superpowers—which is *not* working.

DAVE BARDIN is an illustrator by day and, well, night too. When he's not drawing in his Stronghold of Seclusion, he patrols the streets, protecting the innocent and vanquishing evil. Strangely, the source of his powers is also his one weakness— *mashed potatoes!*